DETROIT PUBLIC LIBRARY

3 5674 05204288 5

P9-DEY-083

CHASE BRANCH LIBRARY
17731 W. SEVEN MILE RD.
DETROIT, MI 48235

Sugar would not eat it

by emily jenkins

illustrated by giselle potter

schwartz & wade books · new york

The morning after his birthday, Leo went to play soccer. Walking home, he found a kitten sitting on the steps of his building.

It was small and fluffy, and had an air of confidence about it.

It didn't seem to belong to anyone.

Leo didn't know anything about kittens, and
he didn't know anything about cats.
But this kitten was very cute, and Leo liked it.
And it seemed to like Leo.
He carried it upstairs and named it Sugar.

Sugar took to Leo's apartment very well.
She played with the bead curtain

and attacked a piece of ribbon that was
still on the floor from Leo's birthday
party the day before.

Then she took a nap.

When she woke up, she was hungry.
Leo gave her a slice of leftover birthday cake.
"It's chocolate," he told her, "with blue frosting
roses. I'm letting you have the last piece."
But Sugar would not eat it.

"Yum yum yum!" coaxed Leo, dipping his
finger in the frosting. "Oooh, delicious."
But Sugar would not eat it.

"Why don't you give it a try?" asked Leo. "How do
you know you don't like it if you don't even *taste* it?"
But Sugar would not eat it.

And so they sat, Sugar staring at Leo and Leo
staring at Sugar, for a very long time.

Leo went out the door and across the hallway. There was his friend Ezra, trying to fix the sink.

When I was small, my dad always told me to drink my milk or I wouldn't grow up big and strong.

"Don't you want to eat your cake so you can grow into a big strong cat?" Leo asked Sugar. "If you don't eat, you can't grow. You'll just be a puny little kitten forever."

But Sugar would not eat it.

Leo went out the door and downstairs to the doughnut cart. There was Jimmy, making a fresh pot of coffee.

COFF

When I was small, and I wouldn't eat my meat loaf, my mama always got so mad because all afternoon, she'd been slaving over a hot stove.

"It took me two hours to bake this cake," Leo told Sugar, "and another hour to do the frosting roses. All that, and now you're not interested? Who do you think I am, the maid?"

But Sugar would not eat it.

Leo went out the door,
downstairs, and up the block.
There was his neighbor
Harriet, doing her crossword
puzzle on the stoop.

When I was small,
my grandma always
told me I couldn't
leave the table
until I finished
all my broccoli.

"Now, Sugar," said Leo. "You are not leaving this table until you eat up all that cake. We can sit here until it's dark outside, I don't care."

But Sugar would not eat it.

The next day, Leo went out the door, downstairs, up the block, and around the corner into the Laundromat.

There was Alice, watching the clothes go around in the washer.

When I was small, my father always told me about children going hungry in other parts of the world.

"Sugar!" shouted Leo. "Children and kittens are hungry in other parts of the world! We do not let perfectly good cake go to waste in this house!"

But Sugar would not eat it.

Leo went out the door, downstairs, up the block, around the corner, past the Laundromat, and into the park. There was Binkie, sitting on a bench and reading the paper.

When I was small, my parents always told me four bites. At least four bites, or I was going to see it again at dinner time.

FUNNY PAGES

"Okay, I'll give you a break," Leo told Sugar. "Just four bites. Four bites and then you can be done. Otherwise, you're going to see this cake again before you get anything else."

But Sugar would not eat it.

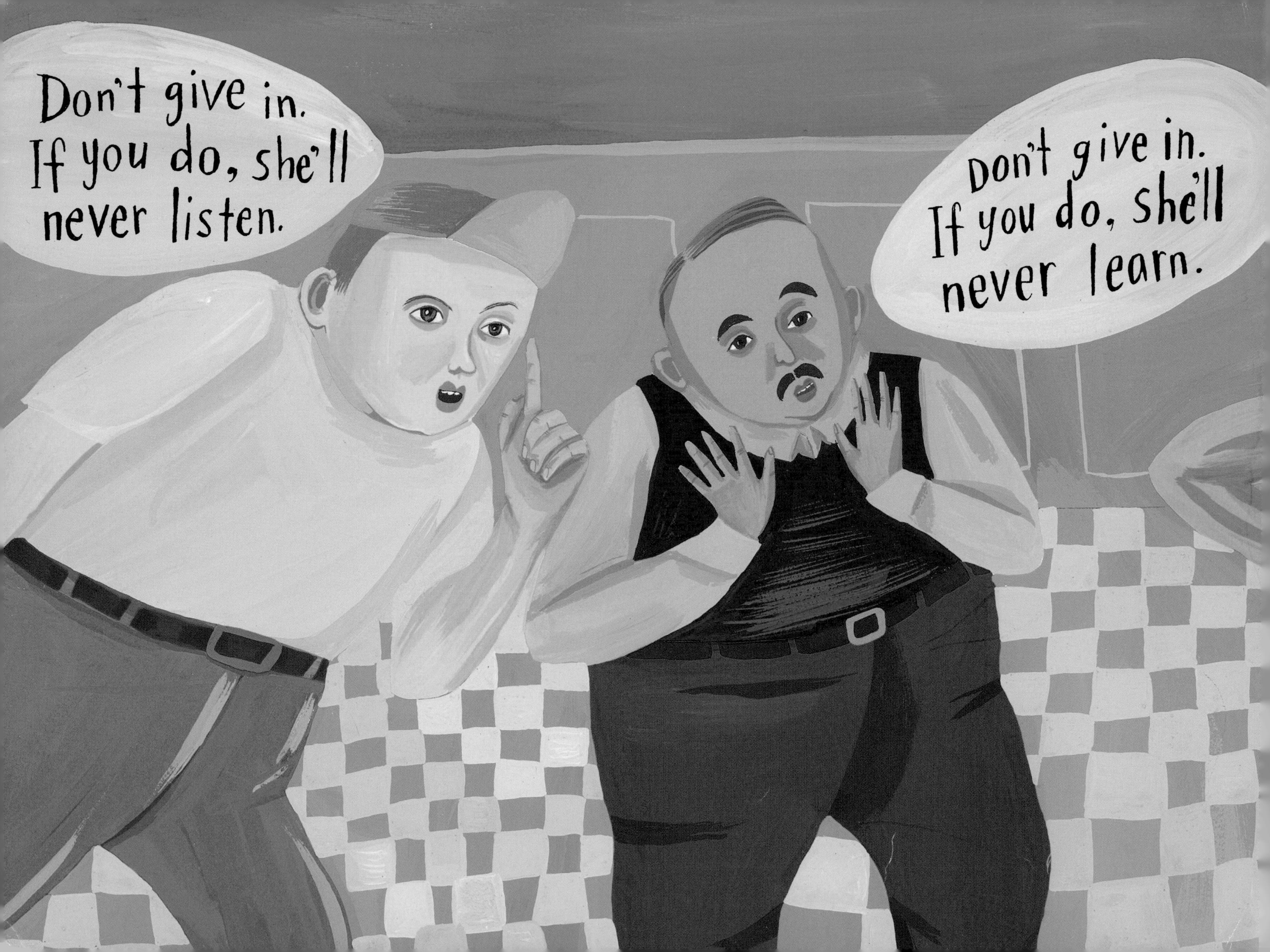

Sugar meowed, and Leo knew she was hungry.
"Eat it, then," said Leo.
But Sugar would not eat it.

"Eat it!"

But Sugar would not eat it.

"Eat it!

Eat it!

EAT IT!"

Leo screamed at her.
But Sugar would not eat it.

She just looked at him.
Sad and hungry, hungry and sad.

Leo began to cry. He didn't know what to do. He loved Sugar, and he hated to see her so unhappy—but how were they going to live together when she wouldn't listen to him and she wouldn't learn?

When he was finally done crying, Leo wiped his nose and splashed some water on his face. He felt hungry, so he went into the kitchen and poured himself a glass of milk and made himself a chicken sandwich.

Suddenly, there was Sugar, up on the counter.

Sugar stuck her head right down into
Leo's glass and began lapping up the milk.
"No, no, Sugar," Leo almost said—but
Sugar was purring.
She looked so happy that he just stood
there and watched her drink.
She drank and drank.

Then she ate some of the
chicken out of Leo's sandwich.

Leo finished what was left,
and ate the cake for dessert.

Sugar went to sleep in his lap.

The next day, Leo bought
Sugar some cat food.

And then he decided to give her a bath.

for Ivy, a good eater
—E.J.

for Isabel, who if she could
would only eat chocolate cake
—G.P.

Published by Schwartz & Wade Books,
an imprint of Random House Children's Books,
a division of Random House, Inc., New York.
Text copyright © 2009 by Emily Jenkins
Illustrations copyright © 2009 by Giselle Potter
All rights reserved.
Schwartz & Wade Books and colophon are trademarks of Random House, Inc.
Visit us on the Web! www.randomhouse.com/kids
Educators and librarians, for a variety of teaching tools, visit us at www.randomhouse.com/teachers
Library of Congress Cataloging-in-Publication Data
Jenkins, Emily · Sugar would not eat it / Emily Jenkins; illustrated by Giselle Potter.—1st ed. · p. cm. · Summary: When Leo adopts a cat, he
names her Sugar and tries to feed her a piece of his birthday cake, but no matter what Leo does to try to make her eat it, the cat simply refuses.
ISBN 978-0-375-83603-9 (trade)—ISBN 978-0-375-93603-6 (lib. bdg.) · [1. Cats—Fiction. 2. Food habits—Fiction.]
I. Potter, Giselle, ill. II. Title. · PZ7.J4134Su 2009
[E]—dc22 · 2007035245
The text of this book is set in Mrs. Eaves.
The illustrations are rendered in pencil, ink, gouache, gesso, and watercolor.
Book design by Emily Seife
MANUFACTURED IN MALAYSIA
1 3 5 7 9 10 8 6 4 2
First Edition
Random House Children's Books supports the First Amendment
and celebrates the right to read.